Running Wild

Lilia Chippendale

DEDICATION

I would like to dedicate this book to Jolly. One of my favourite ponies, she is very precious to me and even though I do not ride her anymore she still means a lot to me.
The reason I dedicated it to her because she has not only helped me while getting my confidence in riding but is also a great friend.

CONTENTS

.

ACKNOWLEDGMENTS

My mother, Hannah, for being such a help with this book, it made me feel so great when the book was finally finished, for the typing part at least. Then I need to thank, Mr. Milne who helped copy and paste it and Mrs. Hugo, who let me stay in at lunch times to choose my fonts and size of my novel. Last but not least, Mr. Marsh who gave me helpful support and comments.

1

The crystal snow glinted in the night's foggy sky. The fresh crisp air whipped around the snowfall. The ground was feathery and soft but sharp, in a pleasant kind of way. The snowy owls made a tooting noise and the weasels scuttled along the snow that crunched when they leapt. The moon was just shimmering behind the heavy snowfall. Up on a cliff, a creamy horse struggled to her feet. She had small fluffy ears that swayed from side to side. She was petite with a rotund body. Glimmering black eyes sat on the sides of her head. She shifted her weight uncomfortably. A wet and skinny foal lay beneath her. He had a dappled grey coat. It was shaking and snorting. His long ears sagged on each side of his soft head.

"Thistle," said Winchester, the creamy mare. "This will be your name," she said soothingly.

Those first few hours passed slowly and Thistle was still finding out how to get to his feet. During that time Thistle wanted to get closer to his mother. He was encouraged to walk, as his mother helped him to his feet. He wobbled ever so slightly, until his legs collapsed and he slumped on the ground. Winchester urged him up again.

His mother looked around pleasantly and waited patiently while he sniffed her large body. Her moon black eyes glistened through the shimmering night sky. Her light furry face blended into a perfect painting with the background of the cave's entrance; the crispy ice chips floating around the navy blue sky.

Thistle almost dozed off immediately that night. He was cuddling up to his mother in complete silence. Winchester admired her little colt and nuzzled him with great pleasure and she too slept through the icy night. The wind still whipped and the snow still whirled around and the weasels still scuttled and the owls still tooted. But to Winchester, everything had changed; nothing was like the first night with your newborn foal, everything was focussed on the sweet furball that lay beside you. It almost seemed as though she was smiling as she nestled up next to her little boy.

The next morning, Thistle woke up to find his mother outside the cave, chewing up all of the grass that she could possibly find amongst the now melting snow. There wasn't much compared to what she needed to keep strong. Winchester walked around for an eternity looking for food and water to feed herself on but all had vanished; there was nothing left.

Hours passed and she still hadn't found anything close by.

"Thistle, dear. We had better search somewhere else, there is no food here," Thistle pricked his ears and walked up to his mother's side.

"Mother, can you smell something? Something like,... Horses!!!" He looked down the valley and saw a praline bay pony feeding on some sweet grass and a lovely golden colt just swishing it's shaggy silver tail back and forth. His face had a glittering white blaze running down it. He was stupendously pretty.

"Star! Star!" Winchester galloped down the hill and up to the bay pony. The bay mare turned around and half reared at the site. She too, galloped off towards her long lost friend.

"Winchester, where have you been?!" exclaimed the bay horse.

"I have been looking after Thistle," said Winchester. Thistle, who could now stand steady and hobble around beside his mother, peered his little head around from behind her.

"It seems, we have both been busy; This is Thunder," said Star. She gestured to the plucky golden colt standing beside her. Winchester stared at him in admiration. Thunder's eyes were a deep blue, a bit like Thistle's. The two horses kept on talking about the things that had happened in the past few weeks whilst the foals crept up behind each ones mother.

"Winchester, do you think we should head to a different place?" asked Star, who was getting anxious.

"Do you mean, go back to.... to Eiskit?" Winchester was planted to the ground.

"Of course!" said Star in exhilaration.

"Okay. But please don't let anything happen to Thistle,"

"Winchester, if I were truly worried then I would have stayed here until a passing herd came. Now let's get over the other side of the lake by the end of the day as there should be more grass," replied Star with confidence.

2

As they walked along, their shoeless hooves made a soft squelching sound, bouncing on the springy damp grass. The squishy lush noise made them shudder as they walked onto it, making it feel like being able to walk on water.

They had been walking all day in an attempt to find Eiskit who would most often be found in the Grange's Hills at this time of year. Soon enough the mothers and foals, despite regular breaks, were getting tired; it was time for them to sleep and it wasn't a pleasant night. There was thunder crashing and falling tree branches. Fortunately, the rocky overhang of the mountain covered them enough so they stayed dry and warm.

Early next morning, they started off to their destination, the herd. Once they had crossed an enormous field they got to a wide track of fresh, shoeless hoof prints. "Eiskit's herd," they said quietly, having recognised his distinctive scent immediately. As quickly as the foals could go, Star and Winchester trotted behind a troupe of Brumbies, trying not to be spotted, as they attempted to follow the tracks of the previous herd to pass through. At the thump of one of their hooves on a hard piece of ground, a roan mare in the Brumby herd, slowed down, was flicking her ears back and forth and she caught a glimpse of them. She gave a great whinny to her fellow mares, they all started to get frisky and jumpy. Luckily, Star saw a path to the left, which Eiskit's herd had apparently taken and drove the four of them towards it, hoping to escape. The little ones were slipping on the muddy bank. "Off to the Grange's Hills!" cried Winchester.

Once safe, they quietly walked towards a tiny valley of hills to find a chestnut coloured horse gleaming in the sun. The stallion was surrounded by some bright mares, some with foals, some without. But he gave a roaring cry when he saw them and came running towards them with his beautiful silver streaked mane blowing behind him.

"Hello," he bellowed, nuzzling the two mares.

"You look lovely today," cried Winchester

"I see you have brought some little ones with you, what are their names?!"

"Thunder and Thistle,"

"They shall be great additions to the herd, unlike the chestnut over there,"

They giggled but suddenly looked stern.

"Needle," he heard his mother say.

That night it rained heavily and the foals were not comfortable and wailed in pain when the chestnut yearling named Thorn, lay upon their bellies. His frightful face showed a curling blaze coming down rather oddly. He was massive compared to the other foals and yearlings.

Winchester had known Eiskit for a long time and knew that he would soon get itchy feet and want to move the herd on to a new pasture. That morning, Thunder and Thistle saw two American horses in the herd talking to each other hastily. It was the chestnut yearling and his mother. They were discussing the increase of horses in other herds and that Eiskit had made a big mistake, he did not know what they meant as in a mistake but herd his mother say.

"I hate that pair," whispered Winchester.

"Detest them!" blurted Star, a little too loudly. The three mares had grown up together and so Winchester and Star were getting tired of the filthy words she spoke. Everyone in the herd suspected Thorn would turn out to be just like his rotten mother, Needle. Thorn's mother, like him, had inherited a deep chestnut coat of fur which her father had had too.

Over the next couple of days, Winchester and Star taught Thunder and Thistle how to sense the tracks of your herd and others and how to avoid slipping and making big tracks. As this would prove to be invaluable in the future. Thistle watched the yearlings gallop along the field and longed to be doing the same. Thorn was there too, he seemed to be kicking the feeble ones to try and get to the front. They stayed at Grange's Hills for a while and the pair of them, being only five days old, enjoyed cantering slowly alongside their mothers down the stream path. Thistle's favourite part was the water, in which he could splash around joyfully.

When the sun rose, a pinch of feathery snow was falling from the sky. The long stretch of grassy ground was no more and was patched over by a thick layer of white fluff.

"Bruhhh!" Thunder was troubled. "What is this mother?" he asked. He was unsure, as on the day he was born, he was on the side of the mountain which faced less extreme weather, so he had never experienced it before.

"It is called snow, nothing to be afraid of," said Star, reassuringly.

Over the week it was harder and harder for the horses to find food. The snow fell more and harder than ever! The whole herd made a fuss that each one's young was catching cold.

"It is a tough winter Eiskit do you think we shall be able to give enough for the young?" Said a nimble black mare, named Hartlin, who apparently cared more about others foals than herself!

"I will find a way," Eiskit snapped. Finally, he decided to try and find a suitable area in which his mares wouldn't have to suffer.

"Mares, I would like to tell you that I shall be going out tonight with Hartlin to find some place elsewhere for us to graze," Then he bowed his head and with a whip of his tail he disappeared into the night.

During Eiskit's absence the mares became weary and the yearlings weak. Most had given up hope except for two, Star and Winchester. They were absolutely certain that Eiskit would make it back. He would do anything he could to save his mares from dying.

It took a while before they came back but by the time a figure approached there was only one, Hartlin was missing.

"Where is Hartlin?" they all questioned.

"Hartlin, couldn't come back. The journey was tough and we ran into trouble with 'you know who'. I was too weak to argue and Hartlin was helpless so she will remain with his herd until we can help her back. I have good news though, lower down in the valley, Spring is almost there. Tomorrow we set off for Capsey Gorge,"

Star and Winchester were speechless. "Do you really think he could mean a Phantom?" gasped Star

At sunrise they set off cautiously for Capsey Gorge. They stopped in a meadow where the rich spring grass was starting to appear and the whole herd were feeling optimistic for the first time in a while. There were birds flying ahead, another sure sign that springtime was on its way. In France the snow usually melted quickly after the winter but whilst it was winter time it filled the Pyrenees in a great big soup of whiteness. Darkness was creeping over the land and the sun was setting extremely quickly.

As they walked into an open area, Thistle gasped as it was packed with large amounts of water and grass! No snow, no snow at all, in fact there was only a small wedge of ice around a pond. Thunder stormed forward to Thistle as he was at the very back of the herd with his mother.

"Isn't it marvellous?!" cried Thunder

"I've seen much better," argued Thorn.

"We didn't ask for your opinion," blurted Thistle as he stood up to Thorn.

Thistle loved the way the mountains bent into the meadow slightly, it made him jump with excitement every time he looked up and around at the view. It was gorgeous.

Rather suddenly, a horse had arrived at the Gorge. He had brought three American light grey mares, a Pinto pony, a chestnut filly and one other which they all recognised as, Hartlin! Most of these mares, including Phantom, were descendants of Kentucky horses, Winchester knew this as her father told her that a foreign farmer shipped over a bunch of American horses to release to the wild. Thistle kept thinking of what Winchester had said about 'you know who' and wondered if this could be him. He didn't get to sleep quickly that night, he forced his eyes shut as he did not want to see anything bad right now, he had a feeling Winchester would tell him when he woke up. It took a while before Thistle finally got to sleep as he was too busy worrying about Phantom. His dream was exceptionally odd that night as no pictures formed in his head, only a voice kept muttering in his head.

"I will get her,"

"I will kill him for this,"

"I will get her back, one day. One day," it went away but Thistle was very disturbed.

3

As Thistle woke up he found the sun rising behind the mountains quietly, as did many other foals and yearlings, except for Thorn. He was chasing the poor fillies and colts away. Instantaneously words shot out of Thistle's mouth. "Cut it out Thorn!" Thorn squealed with happiness. A slight smirk spread across his delighted face.

"If you want me to stop then you'd better stop me yourself," he bellowed.

"Argh!" Thistle shrieked, he suddenly remembered the dream he had had last night. It had all felt so real, the voice. That voice. It was Thorn's. Thistle now believed he had nothing to worry about, as Thorn was all talk and just a bully but nothing more.

On that very same day, Thistle and Thunder were brewing up a plan, only small but to get at Thorn for chasing the colts and fillies. The pair stood soundlessly as they watched Thorn take advantage of a bay yearling. The two were about to crash forward and chase Thorn away as a pack of horses flooded into the Gorge, lead by Phantom. His maroon brown eyes flared as he charged at Eiskit. Phantom made a strong sounding squeal as he thrashed his body attempting to nip his withers, but he failed as Eiskit threw out his hind quarters and twisted his body round to get a grip on Phantom's stocky neck. They were grabbing each other, lashing out with their teeth and kicking each other without mercy, sending blood streaming down each other's faces. Eiskit strived to get a hold on Phantom's muzzle as he reared and landed on Phantom's forehead. The sight was unbearable. Thistle tried to look away but he couldn't, it was frightening. Then, just as Thistle thought that Eiskit would win the battle, Phantom leaped up again and pressed his hooves on top of the beautiful horse's body. Normally, Eiskit would have been able to maintain another horses weight but Phantom was solid in stature. As Eiskit's body dropped to the floor the herd gasped in terror. Thistle lunged forward just in time to hear him say.

"Thistle, be a good boy," then his head flopped and his fit muscular body now sagged on the damp, blood stained floor.

"Oh Eiskit, this was just an accident waiting to happen, silly billy," Thistle's head shot up, it wasn't Thorn's voice, it wasn't Thorn's voice at all that he had heard last night. It was Phantom's voice. He should have known, he could have warned Eiskit and none of this would have happened. Now all because of him he would never see his father again. He had only known him for a couple of weeks and yet in front of him was his father's dead body.

Phantom stood with pride in his victory and started rounding up the mares with his fierce black head but Winchester kept her body where she was, looking down at the dead father of her child and leader of her herd. Her nostrils stopped flaring and her ears started to drop. She sniffed at Eiskit's throat.

Too soon the ground started roaring and rumbling under their feet and Winchester's body suddenly rose to look at what was happening. Two horses carrying something on their backs approached at great speed.

"Run Thistle! Run!" cried Winchester.

Thunder joined him as Winchester sprang over to get Star who was cowering behind a cave. She and Winchester instantly recognised the things on their backs as humans. They had been captured by men as yearlings and were now very anxious of them. Thistle didn't know who these strange things were but right now, he had to run. When Winchester caught up with Thistle and Thunder she looked as though she had just run a marathon! Her face was sweaty and hot and her nostrils were flaring madly with blood trickling out of them.

"What will happen now that Phantom has run away?" Cried Thistle.

"We will have to go with the rest of the herd who escaped. For now we stick together," explained Winchester.

4

Months passed and Thistle was becoming a brave little colt. Thunder was too, his pretty silver mane was glowing in the sunshine and Thistle's dappled grey coat glimmered full of health. His long legs were becoming larger and his face was growing bigger and bolder. His grey ears were now great fly swatting machines. Now the two buddies could easily outrun Thorn who had also managed to escape Phantom, although Thorn was still an extremely strong yearling. He was about to turn two and Thistle and Thunder were barely one.

Now, without his favourite fillies to annoy, Thorn picked on the two more than before. All of the foals that Thorn enjoyed pushing about had been taken by Phantom. Thistle got angry about Thorn's tricks but one day Thunder and Thistle had really had enough. It was on a fine Autumn's day when they decided they were going to get at him. It was late in the evening and most of the mares were feeding on the grass next to their manly yearlings. Some were a year older than Thistle, most of which were nearly ready to leave their mothers.

The two best buddies started hatching a plan quietly in an abandoned wooden shed. Thunder fumbled around with the earth beneath him whilst Thistle kept on coming up with over the top plans, such as; chasing him off a cliff or trying to trick him into the lake. In the end, they decided to go with the eighth idea.

Chasing him far away from the herd, they knew Needle would never have taken much of her time to have taught Thorn how to find his way back. They soaked up the last of the evening sun before collapsing into a heap on the ground.

With the sun rising, Thistle opened his eyes pathetically. His grey coat was matted in brown dust. This was it, the time that they had been waiting for, they would get Thorn. They hoped that their mothers would have a good day and wouldn't worry about them being gone. Going as quickly as they thought possible Thunder and Thistle raced to the pond where Thorn was. Big clouds of dust formed behind their floating hooves. Thistle's gleaming grey body was still in need of growth but his hooves were nearly full size so it made it more difficult to keep quiet as they clopped wherever he went. They watched Thorn calmly as his chestnut body rolled around lazily. He turned around to see where the noise was coming from. Thistle could see that Thorn was outraged when he saw them. He leaped up and attempted to kick Thunder.

He started to chase them, their taunting had the desired effect, as his big bloated body trailed behind them. Galloping out of Capsey Gorge they realised Thorn started to slow down. He obviously didn't have much stamina. But then, he pushed and sprung with his powerful hindquarters and nearly caught up with them. Noticing a lonely forest, Thistle urged Thunder towards it, now Thorn really started to charge. He looked like an angry bull in a Mexican bull-ring. Into the forest they went, when they finally got in, darkness swept over them. It was pitch black. The two friends became separated.

Thistle was frightened out of his skin! He heard horrible stories about horses going into forests and never coming back, and he had hoped never to be in that situation. Suddenly, he thought his plan was nothing but a putrid idea. A swarm of wasps hurried over to him. He tried to shake them away but their sting was vicious. He wailed in agony as he could no longer take it. His eyes began to close and his feet were trembling madly. Then Thistle didn't see the next thing coming either. A square-on kick from Thorn's hind legs swept Thistle off his feet in seconds.

"Boom!" he collapsed onto the floor.

5

"Thistle, Thistle! Are you okay?" cried a voice.

"Thrun?" it seemed as though Thistle had gone mad, he couldn't even say his best friends name right!

Thunder lay beside his befuddled friend and licked his mane kindly.

"Where am I?" said Thistle.

"On the edge of the forest," said Thunder, who had summoned Winchester when he realised his friend must be in trouble. Thunder told Thistle all about the last few hours. With Star's help, Winchester and Thunder had managed to move him to a more open space. Thorn had turned back home as soon as he had delivered his blow to Thistle, having worked their plan out early on. Thistle and Thunder were not looking forward to facing him and his Mother.

Thistle thought back to last night, it was terrible. He could barely remember anything from the forest. The only thing he could think of was when the wasps came, as he turned to lick his swollen wounds. The upside was that Thorn seemed to have had a fright at least and was not bothering them or the fillies at all. Thistle lay on the ground helplessly.

Once Thistle had almost fully recovered, his mother took him out for a slow stroll, just the two of them. He felt a bit agitated as Thunder wasn't there to talk to him but at least, Winchester was. She spoke calmly and was well mannered at all times. But Thistle was young and agile. He wanted to run as fast as he could.

"Mother, can we go for a run?!" he would say.

His lumps were still burning but his head was ready for adventure. He held his tail high, trying to imitate his calm mother.

At the top of the mountain Thistle looked over the ledge. He was surprised to see that his mother had taken him so far away from Capsey Gorge. Thistle wandered back into the sunlight alongside his mother. They were joyfully prancing on the mountain as they knew this was nearly the last of the sunlight.

"Race you!" shouted Thistle, his mother was quick but finally ran out of steam and walked calmly beside her son who was rather slow as he was still in pain. Winchester's ears pricked as she saw something.

"P-people?" Squeaked Winchester. Something was moving in the bushes behind them. Thistle started to fall back on his hind legs with his ears flicking way back to his shaggy mane. His eyes flared around in his eyelid.

But when it jumped out of the bushes it wasn't a person at all, it was a little grey weasel. It limped across the mountain, Winchester watched it eagerly then gave it a little nudge with her nose. It stood on its tippy toes to bring it's front legs onto Winchester's fluffy head. It took one glance at her face and scuttled away making a crackling sound. This episode just brought home to them both, how they were still on edge since Phantom had attacked the herd. They headed back to Capsey Gorge but Thistle now knew that this would not be his home forever.

Winchester woke him up in the morning urging him to get up. Raindrops splattered onto his back. Pain struck through his un exercised legs. His swollen wasp bites started to fade. Thunder decided to give a playful buck to encourage Thistle to play, Thistle couldn't resist. Even though his scabs were hurting he went out to join his best friend. They chased each other round and round for ages until Star called to Thunder. Thistle could hear the two of them whispering to each other but couldn't quite work out what they were saying. Then, by the look on Thunder's face, Thistle knew. Winchester and Star thought they were old enough to move away and make their own herds. Tears filled his eyes, whereas he knew Thorn had been very proud when he had heard that he would be leaving his mother. Thistle did have a dream that sometime he would become the greatest stallion ever known, but now that it was really happening he didn't know whether he wanted to leave or not. It would be lovely to get away from Thorn but it would mean never seeing his mother again, unless of course he was lucky to bump into her. Winchester looked at him with pride and sadness.

6

They were strictly told to go to bed early as they had a big day ahead of them. The two mares watched over their little yearlings whilst letting them snooze away. In the meantime Thistle was dreaming of a faraway land where Thunder stayed beside him as they looked over their mares. Their last night in Capsey Gorge, the owls hooted unpleasantly. The rocky cave creaked as it was just holding up the boulders on top of the stone panels.

"Goodbye mother," sobbed Thistle. He hung his grey neck on her back.

"Goodbye dear," Said Winchester with a twinkle in her eye.

"You two, stay close to each other, don't ever lose each other," Said Star sternly. It wasn't too bad for Thistle, as Thunder was coming with him. He would stay with him for as long as possible. One day he would have to leave Thunder to form his own herd.

By sunlight, Thistle went quickly, with Thunder on his tail. He was obliged to stay in front because Thorn was with them having set off on the same day. He kept scowling and prancing at them. His chestnut ears were forcing themselves farther back than ever. He was the most vicious horse Thistle had ever seen, except for Phantom. Thistle started to wonder where Phantom was because he had only seen him once since Eiskit's death. When he had been in a further away valley, luckily he hadn't seen the two of them.

Thunder and Thistle ventured on and soon enough Thorn was getting bored of them and trailed away more and more each day. They were staying in the grounds of an ancient herd Winchester had once told him about. There was a small shelter in which they stayed. Thorn must have found somewhere to stay because every day they walked to the river they saw him pottering around the grounds of Phantom. It was muggy and wet, but they had to cross over so that they could eat and drink. Thorn would often choose to ignore them, but Thistle often had other ideas. He would spring out at Thorn, instigating a mini fight. He found it fun to wind Thorn up and provoke him, as he was much less confident since the episode in the forest.

One morning Thistle woke up and trotted along with Thunder in front of him. They found Thorn below them on a ledge. Urging him to come up to their level, Thorn swung his head viciously. He emerged to their layer of ground, then pranced and let out a deep whinny. A black horse thundered up the valley replying to his cry. Thistle recognised that face instantly, as Phantom appeared. He charged at Thunder, Thistle did not know why or how Thorn could have got another stallion on his side. Winchester had told him that it was impossible. Thunder fled away from Phantom, who was still chasing him up the valley.

"Thorn! This is ridiculous!" screamed Thistle.

"You don't get it, do you?" he said slyly.

"Don't get what? How could you have got

Phantom on your side?" he bickered on until Thorn replied .

"You see, I was not born as Eiskit's son, my mother was taken by Phantom when the two of them were young. I was born in Phantom's herd, Thistle. I'm his son. But then of course, Eiskit had to ruin it by offering a safe place which my mother couldn't refuse, when I was a small colt. All this happened very soon before you were born. I am surprised your mother didn't tell you. Of course, I must say she is rather daft," he finally stopped and Thistle was burning with both anger and shock.

It explained everything. Now it all made sense. Eiskit had never liked Thorn and his mother quite as much as the others. They both looked different from the herd. Phantom must have come into the Gorge for Needle and his son! The whispering in his ear, "her" was Needle! Phantom wanted to get her back! Thistle realised that if he found Thunder he would be able to tell Phantom where to find Needle and this may calm him. But it wasn't going to be easy, he would have to find Thunder first and of all the places Phantom could take him it could be years until he saw his friend again.

"Where is Thunder?" he Griped.

"How should I know? Phantom will have him by now," he continued. Thistle swished his tail in the air and went storming up the hill.

"Where d'you think your going?" Asked Thorn, then he rushed after Thistle sending a few rocks cascading down the hill.

7

Thistle wandered up to a grove of trees where he could rest the night before continuing his way on to find Thunder. Thorn had returned to what horses called The Dark Horse's Land. He had grown tired of chasing Thistle around the bushes and up and down valleys. He had found no sign of Thunder or his traces, although the whiff traveling to his nose was a very familiar one. With a second's thought he realised it was Winchester's! She could help him find Thunder! With his feet barely touching the ground he set out in search of his Mother. The whirling wind stung his eyes like a thousand bees. The snow prickling his coat constantly. He saw a trail of hoof prints in front of him which he assumed to be Winchester's. He galloped quickly as he followed the faded hoof prints, they were disappearing too fast.

It was hours before the sun came up again, Thistle was shattered.

"Will it ever end?" He asked himself, he was staring down a hill into a valley. Most of the hoof prints were now in squishy mud. Winchester had obviously carried on walking when the snow started to melt. Although Thistle was physically tired his sense of hope did not drop. The smell was getting so much stronger, he ran down the hill still following it. But suddenly, it was combined with at least twenty other different scents. Some familiar, others not but when he turned around he saw the horse he had been looking for. Winchester was happily grazing with Star, even though he was tempted, he held himself back. Phantom was there! He could not be seen by him because he might decide to chase him away just as he had done with Thunder. Thistle assumed that Phantom had captured them. Even though he tried his best not to be seen, Winchester must have recognised her son because she trotted up to him, her graceful head glancing around to make sure no one except Star saw her; who was also trotting behind her.

"Mother, what happened to you?!" Asked Thistle.

"Phantom captured us shortly after you had left. Thistle, how are you?" cried Winchester.

"I am fine, except for the fact that Thunder was taken somewhere by Phantom!" He said sternly.

"M-m-my baby?" sobbed Star, her ears falling backwards.

"I am guessing you haven't seen him?" asked Thistle.

"Not exactly," said Winchester slowly, "but, there was a figure moving through the woods last night. It was a stallion about your age and the same colour as Thunder. Oh, and Thistle, I need to tell you something. It-it's about…."

"Thorn?" questioned Thistle.

"You know?!" she squealed. "But whoever told you?"

"Thorn did," he said in a very dull tone. Winchester sighed and gestured for him to go before they were spotted.

"The woods?" He asked himself later that day. He decided to follow Winchester's knowledge to help him find his mate. The woods were extremely dark at night, Thistle wandered to a clearing in the woods where the last of the now drowning sun still remained. That night he did not lay down on the soft grass but stayed locked on his feet on the hard dirt. Sounds echoed through his head all night long. Hours passed unhurriedly and Thistle got restless.

At the first blush of dawn Thistle yawned his way to his typical self as he opened his eyes and softened his knees a little. His ears flickered as something trod along the sticks on the ground. It scuttled around Thistle's hind legs and then it reared up in greeting. It was another weasel. Thistle waved his head back but in confusion. It hurried off so hastily that Thistle did not even get a chance to say hello; let alone ask him about Thunder. Thistle was both stressed and upset, he couldn't find his friend. He knew he couldn't give up but by midday he had searched over half of the forest. His plan to get Thunder and give Needle back to Phantom, was hopeless. Phantom had already caught back the remaining horses from Eiskit's old herd, and he still wanted more.

As the sun set, Thistle had found no sign of Thunder although, he was lucky not to find any prints of strange herds that would try and attack him. He had found a den with spongy grass lying beneath it. He would have a good night's sleep before heading out to try and find his buddy once more.

8

It was weeks before Thistle finally found any sign of his friend. A trail of hoof prints lay on the ground. He followed them hoping with all his heart that they were Thunder's. His stomach lurched at every corner. His nose way up into the stratosphere until, he found himself in front of a river. A bay horse lay the other side. Thistle had no idea whether he would make it across or not, or if it was even Thunder. It had to be him, no other bay horse could have a white crescent moon shape on his forehead. His feet nearly got swept away by the current as he threw his feet into the ice cold water, attempting to help his friend. When Thistle got there Thunder didn't move a muscle, he was breathing but lay on the floor unconscious.

Minutes passed but they felt like hours to Thistle. He had finally found his friend but he could not help him. He tried nudging his face and neck and pulling his tail. Thunder would not budge. Thistle cried for help but no one came, he hadn't expected anyone to but he was just so frustrated. Just as he was about to give up calling for help a rustling sound came from the bushes. He was suddenly worried he had attracted too much attention and Phantom had followed the sound. He waited and listened hoping that the thing in the bushes was just another weasel. It became louder and louder, closer and closer. Then he could just make out a small chestnut filly and behind her a beautiful Pinto pony. The Pinto pony looked round and overweight but Thistle could see a small glinting in her eye. The chestnut was just the same although not as fat and round as the other. Thistle's heart skipped a beat as the chestnut filly walked up to him. She muttered to herself looking at Thunder. She spoke softly and warmly but a slight crack found its way into her voice as she turned to Thistle and asked,

"Uh-did-you-need-help?" Thistle was overcome with joy that these two had come to help. Thistle recognised this chestnut filly and Pinto mare. They were the ones that arrived at the Gorge with Phantom.

"I know what to do," she told him firmly as she went up to the lake and sucked up some water. She trod over to Thunder and spat it on him. Thunder woke and slowly got to his feet. He was so happy, he nuzzled his best friend with a lot of friendly, loving force.

"Hey um, do you think you could tell me your name?" Thistle finally asked the chestnut mare, after a lot of mumbling. She jumped and smiled gracefully.

"I'm Daisy, this is Apache," Thistle's heart lifted as she stared at him joyfully. "And you?" she asked intrigued.

"Thistle," he said. When Apache spoke she had a vague French accent.

Thistle kept asking Thunder whether he was alright or not but Thunder told him he was absolutely fine numerous times.

"Thunder, how did you get away from Phantom?" asked Thistle.

"He kept me tied up for two weeks then one night

I managed to wriggle my legs free. I escaped from the barn but Phantom heard. I can't remember much but we fought until I fell in some water a little down that way," he reached his nose to the right hand side of the stream, "and then I must have blacked out and been washed up here, I am guessing Phantom returned to where ever he came from?" he said.

"I know where he went but did he say anything?" said Thistle slightly irritated.

"Nothing," Replied Thunder.

"Star was worried sick!" he screamed.

"Maybe I should go and see her?" wondered Thunder.

"No Phantom has got her! He captured them," he said rather sternly.

"Vee kno' of a place zat Phantom vill not find us," said Apache in her French accent.

"Yeah, Golden Ridgeway!" chimed in Daisy, "as far as we know we're the only ones that know about it," she said.

The next day they set off for the Golden Ridgeway which Daisy had told him about, so naturally she lead the way.

9

Most of the way they weren't sheltered from the elements, apart from the short distance they walked through old brick ruins with some of the roof still standing. Thistle started bucking rather happily as it started to rain. First there was just a gentle split splat but then the rain started to fall heavier on their backs. Nevertheless they kept on walking, head facing towards the rain.

"Kvik, vee can make it zer!" Apache ran to the right and and leaped over a log fence. Thistle could see that Daisy was afraid so he hauled himself back a little to stay with her. He talked softly to her trying to catch his breath after the short burst of exertion. She pricked her ears a bit and shook her head but Thistle wouldn't let her turn around he pushed her forwards until they were about three metres away from the log fence. Two metres….One metre…..Whack! Daisy had made it over but caught her leg on it, which was bleeding badly. Thunder was far in front them. Daisy looked fine except for the fact that she couldn't put pressure on her hind leg. Thistle found a piece of barbed wire stuck around Daisy's appendage. He started to unravel it from her hurt limb. It was bleeding horribly, she could not put it down on the ground. She hobbled over to an entrance to a low down valley. They went down the sloped path until a patch of flat ground was visible. Daisy found it difficult to get down because of her leg. Thunder was waiting with Apache in the field.

"Ver vere you?" questioned Apache.

Thistle explained to Apache and added, "we must make sure it is soaked immediately". They all hurried Daisy towards a stream which was luckily nearby. Apache urged her in, it was absolutely freezing. Thistle went in too as Daisy looked rather nervous, he could see that her heart was drumming fast and loud and she was clearly holding her breath. He huddled up next to her and was glad to feel her body relax slightly. She put more and more weight on her leg as the minutes passed. The ice cold water had numbed her leg enough for her to give Thistle a splash with her front hooves. He kicked back playfully at Daisy.

"I think we should get out now, we could catch a cold," she said.

"Good idea, I need to talk to Thunder about something anyway,"

They walked out and Daisy asked Thistle what he needed to talk to Thunder about. He told her he didn't know what had happened to Phantom.

"You should ask Apache about Phantom," said Daisy, "She escaped from him you know".

Thistle approached Apache to ask about it. She told him the most interesting things but nothing was as interesting as when she told him about how she had escaped. Thistle's theory was right, Daisy and Apache were the two who he had seen flooding into the Gorge a few months earlier! Thistle did want to get Winchester back but right now that seemed near impossible but having Apache and Daisy with them now gave him hope. Phantom did have Needle though, so he hoped with all his heart that Phantom would not want to come looking for them as well.

They bathed Daisy's leg three times a day for the next week and as soon as it was good enough to move on, they headed straight to the Golden Ridgeway. Thistle was both excited and alarmed when he got there. The field of grass was much bigger than he expected and there was only a little shelter. Still, this gave Thistle more space to run. A stream flowed through the edge of it providing a good, close source of water. Thistle said his name loud and clear, and an echo came streaming back at him. Thunder swished his tail about, admiring the view. Thistle adored this place and even though they came from Phantom's herd, he loved the two mares that had joined them.

10

Summer arrived at the Golden Ridgeway, making the two young stallions understand where the name had come from. With the sun shining over the ridge it cast the most beautiful golden colour onto the surrounding hills.

Thistle was happily grazing when he spotted something coming towards him in the distance. He immediately called for Thunder. The pair galloped towards the two figures, who despite the sunshine reflecting brightly off them, were unmistakably Winchester and Star.

"Phantom, let us go!" shouted Star with glee.

"He got Needle and Thorn back and that was all he had ever wanted, the herd was just being held hostage, now we are free!"

"We had to come and tell you that we were safe. Don't feel the need to accept us into your herd, it's now your own," Said Winchester.

"Are you crazy?!" Thunder and Thistle both shouted in unison. "We should never have left you".

Thistle and Thunder soaked up the smell as they

watched their mothers grazing in the Golden Ridgeway. Thistle danced around Daisy, he felt so content that the mares had brought him to a place where he could live in peace. He finally felt he was home again.

ABOUT THE AUTHOR

Lilia Chippendale wrote this book, she was ten when she published it.

She loves horses, the main reason she decided for her book to be about them. She loves to ride horses and help out in the stables as much as she can. She hopes that this book will please all that love horses.

Printed in Great Britain
by Amazon